The
Whispering Crows

JAISON GEORGE

Foreword

Mystery and crime have always captivated the human mind. The tension of an unsolved case, the pursuit of truth hidden beneath layers of deception, and the relentless chase between a detective and an elusive villain—these elements form the backbone of any great thriller. The Whispering Crows is not just another crime story; it is an intricate web of suspense, betrayal, and the battle between logic and the unknown.

Set in the hauntingly atmospheric village of Dravnika, this novel takes readers deep into the shadows of a seemingly ordinary place, where every whisper carries secrets, and every shadow conceals a mystery. Inspector Roshan Andreus, a determined investigator, finds himself entangled in a chilling series of murders, where the line between superstition and science blurs. Crows—silent witnesses to the horrors—hover over the crime scenes, their presence more than just a coincidence. What follows is a gripping investigation that will test Roshan's limits— physically, mentally, and emotionally. The stakes are high, the clues are elusive, and the antagonist is as formidable as the hero himself. As you turn each page, you will find yourself drawn deeper into a conspiracy larger than it first appears.

What makes this novel unique is not just its unpredictable twists, but the way it blends cutting-edge technology with an ancient, eerie backdrop. The novel doesn't just challenge the protagonist; it challenges the reader to think beyond the obvious, to question everything they believe to be true. Prepare yourself for an electrifying journey through a maze of deception and danger. The Whispering Crows will keep you on the edge of your seat, racing alongside Roshan as he unearths a sinister truth lurking beneath the surface of Dravnika.

Welcome to the chase. —

Jaison George
(Author, The Whispering Crows)

Preface

Storytelling has always intrigued me—particularly when it masterfully blends mystery, suspense, and the deep psychological complexities of human nature. The Whispering Crows was born from a simple yet compelling thought: What if the most unassuming element of nature—crows—became the silent witnesses to an unimaginable crime? And what if, hidden among them, something far more sinister lurked, meticulously observing, planning, and executing with chilling precision?

*This novel is more than just a crime thriller; it is an exploration of both the hunter and the hunted. It delves into the **burden of justice, the fragility of trust, and the darkness that often hides behind familiar faces**. Inspector Roshan Andreus, the protagonist, is not your conventional hero—he is a man weighed down by duty, racing against time, and tormented by questions that seem to offer no clear answers. His relentless pursuit of the truth leads him through a labyrinth of deception, where every revelation only deepens the mystery.*

*Following the publication of my first book, **The Network of Shadows**, I carefully incorporated valuable feedback from readers into this novel. One particularly insightful suggestion came from my son, who proposed the inclusion of illustrations to enhance the reading experience. Visual elements, after all, have the power to immerse readers more* *deeply, helping them visualize the story as if watching a gripping crime thriller unfold on screen.*

*With this in mind, I structured The Whispering Crows to offer an experience akin to watching a **crime investigation movie**, one that captivates and holds the reader's attention for approx. 2.5 to 3 hours—delivering nothing less than the intensity of a cinematic thriller. Every scene, every narrative twist, and every moment of suspense has been carefully crafted to evoke the same adrenaline rush one would expect from an edge-of-the-seat mystery film.*

*Set against the eerie backdrop of **Dravnika**, a place shrouded in mist and haunted by the ominous presence of crows, this novel challenges the very assumptions we hold about crime, justice, and perception. It merges the essence of classic investigative storytelling with a modern, unpredictable twist—designed to keep you guessing until the very last page.*

*For those who crave **a well-crafted mystery**, who revel in **the thrill of the chase**, and who seek **answers in the most unexpected places**—this book is for you.*

I hope The Whispering Crows lingers in your thoughts long after you turn the final page.

— Jaison George
(Author, The Whispering Crows)

Chapter 1: Whispers in the Mist

The mist rolled in thick over the village of Dravnika, curling around the wooden rooftops and the ancient banyan trees like a shroud. It slithered through the narrow alleys, veiling the cobbled pathways and casting an eerie glow over the dimly lit lanterns that still flickered outside homes. The air was heavy, almost oppressive, carrying with it the unmistakable scent of damp earth, mingled with the faint aroma of burning firewood from distant kitchens where early risers prepared their morning meals.

Dravnika was an old village, its history etched into the very walls of its crumbling stone houses and the fading murals on temple walls. The houses, made of laterite bricks and sloping clay-tiled roofs, stood like silent sentinels, their wooden doors adorned with intricate carvings now worn by time. Some homes bore the scars of the past—cracked pillars, moss creeping along the edges, and courtyards where once grand celebrations had taken place but now lay deserted, save for the occasional rustle of leaves swept in by the wind.

The streets of Dravnika were narrow, winding pathways that had seen generations of footsteps, from merchants with bulging sacks to barefoot children playing under the midday sun. The village square, the heart of Dravnika, was slowly coming to life as the first golden streaks of dawn pierced through the mist. Vendors, wrapped in shawls, set up their stalls, arranging fresh produce, handmade trinkets, and bundles of aromatic spices. The tea stalls, already brimming with early customers, released plumes of steam, blending with the cool morning air as conversations of politics, local gossip, and superstitions filled the space.

As dawn broke, the crows began to stir. Their restless cawing shattered the morning stillness, a cacophony that seemed to belong to another world. Black silhouettes perched on rooftops and telephone wires, their beady eyes glinting in the dim light. Some pecked at the grains scattered outside doorsteps, while others circled above the towering temple spire, their cries piercing through the dense fog. For the people of Dravnika, crows were not just birds—they were omens. The elders often whispered of their connection to the departed, claiming that a crow's call at an unexpected hour signified an impending misfortune.

Despite the villagers' deep-rooted beliefs, there was an uneasy stillness in the air that morning, as if nature itself was bracing for something *unseen. The mist seemed thicker than usual, clinging to the trees and obscuring familiar landmarks. A stray dog whimpered as it scurried past the temple steps, its ears twitching at the relentless cries of the crows. The villagers, though accustomed to their presence, couldn't shake off the sense of unease that settled over them.*

It was as if Dravnika itself was holding its breath, waiting for something—or someone—to disturb its fragile silence.

Thomas Chacko, the most powerful man in the village, was found dead that morning. His body lay sprawled in the courtyard of his sprawling ancestral home, his glassy eyes staring into the overcast sky. The crows perched on the walls and rooftops nearby were unnervingly still, their black eyes glinting as they observed the lifeless body. The villagers whispered in hushed tones, their faces pale with fear. The only sound, apart from the occasional caw, was the creak of the rickety wooden gate swinging in the breeze.

Roshan Andreus, freshly transferred IPS officer, arrived at the scene. His arrival did little to calm the villagers. They eyed him with a mix of suspicion and curiosity. To them, he was an outsider, a man from the city who wouldn't understand the ways of Dravnika. Roshan stepped out of the Jeep, his tall frame cutting an imposing figure against the grey sky. His sharp features betrayed no emotion, but his dark eyes scanned the scene with the precision of a predator.

"Who found the body?" Roshan asked, his voice cutting through the murmurs. A constable stepped forward, his expression grim.

"The caretaker, sir. He said he came to deliver tea and found Mr. Chacko lying here. No signs of a struggle."

Roshan nodded and crouched beside the body, his leather boots creaking as he moved. Thomas Chacko's face was frozen in an expression of mild surprise. There were no visible wounds, no blood, no signs of violence. Yet something about the scene felt wrong to Roshan. He glanced at the crows, their silence unnerving. It was as if they were waiting for something.

A constable stood near the doorway, flipping through his notepad. "No signs of forced entry, sir. The main door was locked from the inside. Servants didn't hear anything unusual, except..." he hesitated, looking up.

"Except?" Roshan prompted.

"One of them mentioned hearing crows making a ruckus around midnight. Unusually loud."

Roshan glanced at the crows still perched around the property. Something about their presence felt unnatural. "And what do we know about the victim?"

The constable sighed, flipping to another page. "Thomas Chacko, 58 years old. Former government employee, now retired. Lived alone in this ancestral house. Servants stayed in servant quarters next to the home and usually came back to the house in the morning for household chores. Neighbours say he kept to himself, barely socialized."

A voice interrupted them as a middle-aged woman, identified as Thomas' sister, entered the courtyard. Her eyes were red-rimmed, her hands trembling slightly.

"Inspector, I can't believe this is happening. He was all alone in his final days."

Roshan gestured for her to sit. "Can you tell us anything about him? Was there anyone he was in contact with?"

She wiped her tears. "Not many. He distanced himself from the family years ago. His wife left him, and their children... they don't speak to him anymore. He never talked about it, but we all knew how much it weighed on him."

Roshan exchanged a glance with the constable. A man with no close family, no social ties-isolated. A perfect target. But why him?

"Do you know if he had any enemies?" Roshan pressed.

She hesitated. "I... I don't know. He didn't have many friends. There were times he'd talk about some old disputes, but I never paid much attention."

Roshan nodded, filing away the information. "If you remember anything else, please let us know."

As she left, Roshan turned back to the constable. "A man alone, disconnected from his family. That kind of loneliness makes a person vulnerable."

The constable scribbled in his notepad. "And that makes this even stranger. Who would go after a man who had nothing left?"

"Sir, the villagers are saying it's a curse," the constable said hesitantly. "They believe the crows..."

"The crows didn't kill him," Roshan said curtly, standing abruptly. "Get the forensic team here. I want the entire area cordoned off. And find that caretaker. I need to speak to him."

As the constable hurried off, Roshan's gaze lingered on the crows. They seemed to be watching him, their heads tilting slightly as if in silent judgment. He shook off the feeling and turned to the small group of villagers gathered near the gate.

"You," he called out to an old man who was clutching a walking stick. The man's milky eyes widened in fear as he shuffled forward.

"Yes, sir," the man croaked, his voice trembling.

"What's this about a curse?" Roshan asked.

The old man's hands shook as he tightened his grip on the stick. "The crows, sir," he whispered. "They know. They see everything. When they stop cawing, it means death is near."

"And what did you see last night?" Roshan's tone was sharper now, his patience thinning.

"Nothing, sir. Nothing unusual. But... the crows were here. Just like now. Watching."

Superstition ran deep in Dravnika, and Roshan knew it often clouded rational thinking. Yet the old man's words lingered uneasily in his mind.

Roshan suppressed a sigh. Superstition ran deep in villages like Dravnika, and it often clouded rational thinking. He dismissed the old man with a nod, though his words lingered uneasily in Roshan's mind. He turned back to survey the courtyard. Thomas Chacko was a man of influence, known for his wealth and his disputes with many in the village. His death was not an accident, of that Roshan was certain. But how and why remained a mystery.

Interrogation of the Caretaker:

Roshan found the caretaker, an elderly man named Ravi, sitting on the steps of the servant quarters. His hands trembled slightly as he twisted the end of his dhoti. His eyes, sunken and tired, flickered with an unease that Roshan had seen many times before.

"Ravi," Roshan called, his tone measured. "I need to ask you a few questions."

Ravi stood hastily, nodding. "Yes, sir. Anything you need."

"You were the first to find the body?" Roshan asked.

"Yes, sir," Ravi replied, swallowing hard. "I bring him his morning tea every day. When I walked into the courtyard, I saw him lying there, just... staring up."

"Did you touch the body?"

"No, sir! I swear, I didn't. I ran and called for help."

Roshan studied him for a moment before asking, "Did Thomas Chacko seem worried about anything lately? Did he mention any threats or strange visitors?"

Ravi hesitated, then nodded slowly. "A few days ago, he seemed restless. He would stand in the courtyard at night, looking up at the sky, mumbling to himself. I heard him say something about... shadows watching him."

"Shadows?" Roshan frowned. "Do you mean people? Was someone watching the house?"

"I don't know, sir," Ravi admitted. "But he was afraid. He kept checking the windows, locking the doors himself at night."

Roshan exchanged a glance with the constable. "Did he receive any visitors recently?"

Ravi hesitated again. "Not many, sir. Just one man... a few nights ago."

Roshan's eyes sharpened. "Who?"

"I don't know his name, sir. He came late, around 9 PM. I only saw him from a distance, but he wore white clothes... like a businessman."

Roshan's jaw clenched. "And did you hear anything from their conversation?"

Ravi shook his head. "No, sir. But after that visit, Mr. Chacko barely spoke to anyone. He just looked troubled."

Roshan straightened, his mind racing. "If you remember anything else, even the smallest detail, you come to me immediately."

Ravi nodded fervently. "Yes, sir."

As Roshan turned back toward the house, the weight of this revelation settled over him. A mysterious visitor, an increasingly paranoid victim, and an unnatural silence from the crows. He was beginning to see the threads of a much darker story.

"Inspector," came a voice from behind him. Roshan turned to see Martin, a local agriculturalist. Martin's calm expression and neatly pressed white shirt made him look out of place among the anxious villagers.

"Yes?" Roshan asked, his eyes narrowing slightly.

"Thomas Chacko had many enemies," Martin said, his tone even. "Not everyone in this village is sad to see him go."

"And what about you, Mr. Martin?" Roshan asked, stepping closer. "Are you sad to see him go?"

Martin's lips curled into a faint smile. "Sadness is a luxury not everyone can afford, Inspector. But I will say this—in Dravnika, death is rarely the end of a story."

Before Roshan could respond, Martin turned and walked away, his silhouette disappearing into the mist. Roshan watched him go, a gnawing feeling of unease settling in his chest. Martin's words replayed in his mind: Death is rarely the end of a story.

The forensic team arrived shortly after, breaking Roshan's train of thought. They began their work, combing through the courtyard for evidence. Roshan paced the perimeter, his sharp eyes scanning every detail. He stopped abruptly when he noticed something on the ground near the gate—a single black feather. It was unremarkable, but it felt out of place. He picked it up, turning it over in his hands. The edges were frayed, as if worn down by time or... something else.

"What do you make of this?" Roshan asked the forensic officer, handing over the feather.

The officer examined it briefly before shrugging. "Probably just a feather from one of the crows, sir."

"Probably," Roshan echoed, though his instincts told him otherwise.

The villagers remained clustered outside the gate, their anxious murmurs blending with the occasional cawing of the crows. Roshan noticed a young boy standing apart from the group, clutching a slingshot. He beckoned the boy over.

"What's your name?" Roshan asked, crouching slightly to meet the boy's eyes.

"Arjun, sir," the boy replied nervously.

"Arjun, did you see anything unusual last night?"

The boy hesitated, glancing at the villagers before whispering, "The crows were flying in circles, sir. Just above Mr. Chacko's house. They didn't stop until... until he was found."

Roshan nodded, handing the boy a piece of candy from his pocket. "Thank you, Arjun. Go home and stay safe."

As the boy ran off, Roshan's mind churned with questions. The crows' behaviour was unnatural, but whether it was a clue, or a coincidence remained to be seen.

As the day wore on, the villagers began to disperse, their whispers fading with the mist. But the crows remained. They perched on the rooftops and trees, their black eyes following Roshan as he moved. He could feel their gaze, heavy and unrelenting.

"The crows know... they always know," the old man's voice echoed in his mind.

As Roshan walked back towards his Jeep, his mind reeled. A mysterious visitor, Chacko's growing paranoia, and the eerie silence of the crows—everything seemed connected. Then, a thought struck him. The caretaker's description of the visitor... white clothing, a composed presence. It reminded him of Martin.

A chill crept down Roshan's spine as he considered the possibility. Could Martin have been the last person to see Chacko alive?

As the Jeep rumbled to life, he clenched his jaw. He needed to know more. And if Martin had any connection to this, Roshan was going to find out.

Chapter 2: The Biologist's Observations

The narrow road leading to Khairpur's forest research centre was lined with overgrown bushes and trees, their branches stretching out like skeletal fingers. The centre itself was modest, a brick building with moss creeping along its walls. Shilpa Narayan parked her bike and took a deep breath. Shilpa had always been drawn to the mysteries of nature. she had spent years studying avian behaviour, fascinated by how birds could sense changes in the environment long before humans could. Her research had led her to understand the patterns of flight, migration, and even the subtle warnings animals gave before a natural disaster or an unforeseen event. But while most of her colleagues saw this as purely scientific, Shilpa had always believed there was more to it—a connection between human life and the instincts of the wild.

The air smelled of damp wood and wet grass, a scent she'd grown used to over the years. But today, it felt heavier—perhaps it was the whispers about Thomas Chacko's death that lingered in the back of her mind.

Shilpa adjusted her backpack, stuffed with notebooks and binoculars, and stepped inside. Her small office overlooked the dense forest, a view she usually found calming. On one wall, pictures of various bird species adorned a corkboard, and a large whiteboard held her ongoing notes and observations. She had always found solace in nature, a passion she credited to her father, a retired forest ranger. He had taught her to respect and understand wildlife, instilling in her a fascination for birds, especially crows.

"They're smarter than you think," her father had once said, pointing to a crow perched on their windowsill. "Don't underestimate them, Shilpa. They watch, they learn, and they remember."

His words echoed in her mind now as she unpacked her equipment. Her research assistant, Anand, knocked on the door and entered, carrying a tray with two steaming cups of coffee.

"Good morning, ma'am," Anand said, setting the tray on her desk. "I thought you could use this. Long day ahead."

"Good morning, Anand. Thank you," Shilpa replied, taking a sip of the coffee. "Did you get the reports from the villagers?"

"Yes," Anand said, handing her a folder. "Most of them are saying the same thing. The crows were circling Thomas Chacko's house the night he died. And..." He hesitated.

"And?" Shilpa prompted, raising an eyebrow.

"They're saying the crows are cursed," Anand said, his voice barely above a whisper. "Some of the older villagers believe the crows are harbingers of death."

Shilpa sighed, placing the folder on her desk. "Superstition," she muttered. "Anand, our job is to separate fact from fiction. We'll document their behaviour and look for patterns. If the crows are behaving differently, there's a scientific explanation for it."

"Of course, ma'am," Anand said, though he still looked uneasy.

As they discussed their plan for the day, Shilpa's phone buzzed. She glanced at the screen and saw an unknown number. Frowning, she answered.

"Hello, this is Shilpa Narayan," she said.

"Ms. Narayan, this is IPS Officer Roshan Andreus," a deep voice replied. "I'm investigating the death of Thomas Chacko. I understand you're a wildlife biologist specializing in birds?"

"Yes, that's correct," Shilpa said, sitting up straighter. "How can I help you, Officer?"

"The villagers seem to think the crows had something to do with his death," Roshan said. "I'm hoping you can provide some insight into their behaviour. Are you available for a meeting?"

"I am," Shilpa replied. "When would you like to meet?"

"Today, if possible," Roshan said. "Can you come to the police station?"

Shilpa hesitated. "How about we meet here at the research centre? I can show you some of my observations."

There was a brief pause before Roshan replied. "Alright. I'll be there in an hour."

After hanging up, Shilpa looked at Anand. "Change of plans. We'll start the fieldwork later. For now, let's prepare to meet the officer."

Exactly an hour later, Roshan arrived at the research centre. He stepped out of his Jeep, his expression unreadable as he surveyed the building. Shilpa greeted him at the entrance, extending her hand.

"Officer Andreus, welcome," she said. "Thank you for coming."

Roshan shook her hand, his grip firm. "Thank you for agreeing to meet on short notice," he said. "I'm hoping you can shed some light on this situation."

Shilpa led him inside to her office, where Anand had set up a small table with coffee and biscuits. As Roshan sat down, his sharp eyes scanned the room, taking in the photographs and notes on the walls.

"You have an impressive setup," he remarked.

"Thank you," Shilpa said. "I've been studying birds for over a decade, and crows are one of my specialties. They're fascinating creatures." Roshan leaned forward slightly. "Fascinating enough to kill a man?"

Shilpa chuckled softly. "Crows are intelligent, but they're not murderers, Officer. What exactly do you want to know?"

Roshan pulled out a small notebook. "The villagers claim the crows were circling Thomas Chacko's house the night he died. Is that normal behaviour?"

"It's unusual but not unheard of," Shilpa said. "Crows are highly social and territorial. If there was something unusual happening at his house *it could have attracted their attention."*

"Something unusual like a murder?" Roshan asked, his tone sharp. "Possibly," Shilpa admitted. "But we'd need more evidence to draw any conclusions."

They spent the next hour discussing the behaviour of crows, with Shilpa explaining their intelligence and adaptability. She shared anecdotes about how crows could recognize faces, solve puzzles, and even hold grudges. Roshan listened intently, occasionally jotting down notes.

"One more thing," Shilpa said as their conversation wound down. "I'd like to observe the crime scene myself. Seeing the area might help me understand why the crows were behaving the way they did."

Roshan considered this for a moment before nodding.

"Alright. I'll arrange for you to visit tomorrow. In the meantime, if you notice anything unusual, let me know immediately."

"Of course," Shilpa said, walking him to the door. As Roshan left, she couldn't shake the feeling that their conversation had barely scratched the surface of a much deeper mystery.

As the sun dipped below the horizon, casting long shadows across the forest, Shilpa returned to her office. She looked out the window and saw a single crow perched on a nearby tree, its dark silhouette stark against the fading light. It seemed to be watching her, unblinking.

For the first time in years, Shilpa felt a shiver run down her spine.

Chapter 3: A Silent Witness

The soft hum of activity in Dravnika's police station was shattered by the shrill ring of the phone on Roshan's desk. He picked it up on the second ring, his sharp tone cutting through the noise.

"Inspector Roshan speaking," he said.

"Sir, we've got another one," came the voice of Sub-Inspector Patel. "A retired schoolteacher, Raman Pillai, found dead in his house this morning. Same as Thomas Chacko—no signs of struggle, no visible injuries."

Roshan's jaw tightened as he gripped the receiver. "Location?"

"Near the village temple. We've already secured the area," Patel replied.

"I'm on my way," Roshan said, slamming the phone down. He grabbed his notebook and signalled for the driver. As the Jeep roared to life, Roshan couldn't help but feel a gnawing sense of dread. Two deaths, eerily similar, and no answers.

The temple's bell echoed faintly in the distance as Roshan arrived at the scene. Raman Pillai's modest house was surrounded by villagers whispering in hushed tones. The air was heavy with the scent of incense and damp soil. Roshan stepped out of the Jeep, his presence commanding immediate silence.

"Clear the area," he ordered, gesturing for the constables to push the crowd back. Inside the house, the scene was disturbingly familiar. Raman Pillai lay on his cot, his eyes wide open and staring at the ceiling. The crows, once again, had gathered outside, their black forms casting ominous shadows through the windows.

Roshan's eyes swept the room, searching for anything out of place. His gaze fell on the open window and the faint scratch marks on the sill. He crouched to examine them closely, but they told him nothing definitive. He straightened up, frustration bubbling beneath his composed exterior.

"Patel," Roshan called. The young officer hurried over. "Who found him?"

"The milk delivery person noticed him through the window while making the morning rounds. The door was locked from the inside. Roshan frowned. "No forced entry?"

"None, sir. It looks like the attacker didn't enter the house at all," Patel said.

"Interesting," Roshan murmured. "Bring the neighbour in for questioning. And get the forensic team here immediately."

The neighbour, a middle-aged woman named Lakshmi, sat nervously on a wooden chair in the corner of the house. Her hands fidgeted with the edge of her saree as she avoided Roshan's piercing gaze.

"Lakshmi," Roshan began, his voice firm but not unkind, "I understand you were the first to see Raman Pillai this morning. Can you tell me what happened?"

Lakshmi nodded hesitantly. "I came to deliver milk, sir. Like I do every morning. But today, when I knocked, he didn't answer. I thought he might still be asleep, so I looked through the window. That's when I saw him... lying there."

"And the door?" Roshan asked.

"It was locked from the inside," Lakshmi replied. "I didn't know what to do, so I ran to call the others."

"Did you notice anything unusual before this?" Roshan pressed. "Any noises, visitors, anything out of place?"

Lakshmi shook her head. "No, sir. But..." She hesitated, glancing nervously toward the window.

"But what?" Roshan's tone sharpened slightly.

"The crows," Lakshmi whispered. "They were everywhere. On the trees, on the roof. Just sitting there, watching. It felt... wrong."

Roshan's eyes flicked to the window, where the crows still perched, their black eyes glinting in the light. "Have you ever seen them behave like this before?"

"No, sir," Lakshmi said. "They've been acting strange ever since Thomas Chacko died. It's like they know something we don't."

Roshan straightened, his mind racing. "Thank you, Lakshmi. You've been very helpful." He turned to Patel. "Make sure she's escorted home safely."

As Patel left, Roshan decided to visit one of the key figures in the village: Martin. The agriculturalist, a person of interest. Martin's house was a modest but well-kept structure surrounded by neatly trimmed hedges. Roshan knocked on the door, and Martin himself answered, his calm demeanour unchanged.

"Inspector Andreus," Martin said with a small smile. "What a surprise. Please, come in."

Roshan paused at the entrance, his sharp eyes locking onto Martin. "Hope you are alone here. Can I know about your family, Martin?"

Martin raised an eyebrow but answered smoothly. "My parents live in the village outskirts. They prefer a quiet life away from all this noise. My younger brother works in the city, barely visits." He gestured towards the house. "I like my space, Inspector. Helps me think."

Roshan nodded slowly, noting the ease with which Martin answered. But something about the response felt too rehearsed. He stepped inside, his sharp eyes scanning the room. It was tidy, almost too tidy, with bookshelves lined with volumes on agriculture and technology.

Roshan leaned forward slightly. "Tell me, Martin. A few nights before Thomas Chacko were murdered, a mysterious visitor came to his house.

Witnesses say he wore white, dressed like a businessman. Do you know anything about that?"

Martin let out a light chuckle, shaking his head. "Roshan, you seem determined to connect unrelated dots."

Roshan didn't move. "You're changing the subject. Why?"

Martin's faint smile didn't waver. "Or maybe you're just looking for answers in the wrong places."

Roshan: "You seem to know quite a bit about the village, Mr. Martin. Any thoughts on what's happening?"

Martin's smile didn't falter. "I'm just an observer, Inspector. But I've always believed that in a place like this, secrets don't stay buried for long."

Roshan spoke slowly, his voice deep and measured, carrying a sense of intensity.

"Do you have any secrets I should know about?"

Martin chuckled softly. "We all have secrets, Inspector. The question is, which ones matter?"

Martin's expression remained unreadable, but there was a brief flicker in his eyes—so quick that most would have missed it. He leaned back in his chair, exhaling slowly. "Dravnika is full of visitors, Inspector. Businessmen, traders, officials... I can't possibly know every person who comes and goes."

Roshan narrowed his eyes, watching him carefully. "Strange, isn't it? Chacko seemed disturbed after that visit. He was restless, checking his doors, speaking of shadows. And then he turns up dead."

Martin let out a light chuckle, shaking his head. "Roshan, you seem determined to connect unrelated dots. Perhaps the man was just a debt collector, or an old acquaintance. Not everything is as sinister as you make it out to be."

Roshan didn't move, didn't blink. He could feel it—Martin was avoiding the question, diverting attention elsewhere. His response was too smooth, too calculated.

Roshan clenched his jaw. The conversation had shifted into Martin's control, and he knew pressing further wouldn't get him anywhere. But something about his reaction didn't sit right.

As Roshan left Martin's house, a spark of suspicion had been planted in his mind. Martin's calmness felt deliberate, almost practiced, and his words lingered like a riddle.

The heavy wooden desk shook as Commissioner Menon's fist came crashing down, the sharp sound echoing through the stark, dimly lit office. The papers on his desk fluttered from the impact, and the officers standing near the doorway stiffened. His glare was piercing, his voice laced with barely restrained fury.

"Two deaths, Inspector! Two high-profile villagers dead, and you've given us nothing!" His voice thundered through the room.

Inspector Roshan stood his ground, his posture rigid, his face unreadable, but inside, he felt the weight of the moment pressing hard against him. The air in the office was thick, stifling with tension.

"Do you have any idea what kind of pressure I'm under?" Menon continued, his tone like a whip. He exhaled sharply, rubbing his temple before slamming both hands on the desk, leaning forward, his eyes burning into Roshan's. "The *entire district is looking for answers! The media is hounding me like vultures, and the higher-ups want results!"*

Roshan remained composed, but his jaw tightened. He met Menon's gaze without flinching.

"Sir, the cases are connected. I'm certain of it," he said, his voice calm but firm. "But the method is unlike anything I've seen before. It's methodical, precise. Whoever's behind this isn't leaving a trace. I need more time."

"Time is a luxury you don't have," Menon snapped, straightening up. His anger had not subsided, and the vein on his temple pulsed. He took a deep breath before continuing, his voice dropping to a deadly calm. "The media is already calling this the work of a serial killer. The public is scared. Investors are pulling back from our district. Do you want them to think we're incompetent?"

Roshan's fists clenched at his sides. The accusation stung, but he refused to react emotionally.

"No, sir," he said, his voice steady despite the storm raging inside him. "I will get results."

Menon studied him for a long moment, then exhaled, shaking his head as if he were dealing with a stubborn child. "See that you do," he said coldly. "Or I'll find someone who can."

The finality in his tone sent a clear message—Roshan was on borrowed time.

Roshan didn't respond. He didn't argue. He simply nodded once, turned on his heel, and walked out. His footsteps echoed in the silent corridor, each one carrying the weight of responsibility, frustration, and a steely resolve.

As he stepped outside into the humid evening air, he ran a hand through his hair, exhaling slowly. The tension from the meeting still clung to him, but he refused to let it shake him.

The pressure was mounting. The expectations were suffocating. But Roshan was not a man who buckled under weight—he thrived on it.

Somewhere in Dravnika, the truth was waiting. And he was going to find it—no matter what it took.

Chapter 4: Cryptic Patterns

The relentless hum of Roshan's mind mirrored the steady ticking of the wall clock in his office. The two deaths, Thomas Chacko and Raman Pillai, lingered like a weight he couldn't shrug off. He leaned back in his chair, flipping through his notes. The details were sparse, frustratingly so. No forced entry, no visible signs of struggle, and yet the victims were dead. And then there were the crows.

Roshan's thoughts were interrupted by a knock on his office door. Sub-Inspector Patel stepped in, holding a thick folder.

"Sir, the autopsy report for Raman Pillai just came in," Patel said, placing the folder on the desk. "Same as Thomas Chacko. Cause of death... inconclusive."

Roshan's brow furrowed as he flipped open the folder. The report detailed fluid buildup in the lungs, indicative of asphyxiation, but there was no evidence of any external or internal trauma. It didn't make sense.

"What about toxicology?" Roshan asked, his voice tense.

"Still pending, sir," Patel replied. "But..." He hesitated.

"But what?" Roshan demanded, his sharp gaze locking onto Patel.

"The forensic team found faint traces of what they think might be gas residue near the window," Patel said. "They're running tests to confirm."

Roshan's mind raced. Gas. It was a lead, albeit a thin one. "Good work," Roshan said, closing the folder. "Get me the results as soon as they're ready. In the meantime, I need to speak with Ms. Narayan."

The forest research centre was bathed in the golden light of late afternoon when Roshan arrived. Shilpa was in her office, reviewing footage she had collected from nearby security cameras close to the crime scenes. Her desk was cluttered with notes, sketches, and books on bird behaviour. She looked up as Roshan entered, her expression a mix of curiosity and concern.

"Officer Andreus," she said, gesturing for him to sit. "What brings you here?"

"The investigation," Roshan said, taking a seat across from her.

"We've got a potential lead. Gas residue was found near the window of Raman Pillai's house. I need your thoughts on the crows' behaviour."

Shilpa leaned back in her chair, her brow furrowing. "Gas? That would explain the lack of physical evidence on the victims. But... how does that connect to the crows?"

"That's what I need your help figuring out," Roshan said. "You mentioned the crows behaving strangely. Is it possible they're being used somehow?"

Shilpa considered this for a moment. "Crows are highly intelligent," she said. "They're capable of recognizing patterns, even faces. But manipulating them to this extent... it seems unlikely."

"Unlikely doesn't mean impossible," Roshan said. "Could their behaviour be a reaction to the gas? Something instinctual?"

Shilpa's eyes lit up with interest. "That's a possibility," she said. "Certain chemicals can affect animals differently than humans. If the gas is strong enough to harm a person, it might be triggering a defensive or territorial response in the crows."

"I'll need you to keep observing them," Roshan said.

"Any changes, no matter how small, could be important." "Of course," Shilpa said. "I'll also review the footage I've collected. Maybe there's something I missed."

Later that evening, as Roshan was preparing to leave the station, his phone buzzed. It was Shilpa.

"Officer Andreus," she said, her voice tense. "I've been going through the footage from the cameras near Raman Pillai's house. There's something you need to see."

Roshan's pulse quickened. "What is it?"

"There's a crow," Shilpa said. "It's... different. Its movements are strange, almost unique. It's in the background of several frames, hovering near the window." oshan's grip tightened on his phone. "Send me the footage. I'll look at it tonight."

"I'll email it right away," Shilpa said. "But Roshan... this could be important. It's not natural."

"Understood," Roshan replied. "Good work, Shilpa. Let's talk tomorrow."

Chapter 5: The Third Murder

Roshan's thoughts about the footage were still fresh in his mind the following morning when the call came. Sub-Inspector Patel burst into his office, his face pale and his breath short.

"Sir, we've got another murder," Patel blurted out, clutching a file.

Roshan's stomach dropped. "Who is it this time?"

"Ravi Menon, a journalist," Patel replied, his voice trembling. "He was found dead inside an ATM booth at the junction. Sir... it happened early this morning."

Roshan's eyes narrowed as he set down his tea. "Inside an ATM booth? What was he doing there?"

"Withdrawals, apparently," Patel said. "But the booth... it was sealed shut when the cleaning staff arrived, and he was found unresponsive. No signs of struggle, sir, but it's... unusual."

Roshan grabbed his notebook and car keys. "Let's go. Get Shilpa on the phone. I want her at the scene as soon as possible."

The ATM booth at the junction was cordoned off with yellow police tape, the morning sun casting long shadows across the street. A small crowd of onlookers had gathered, whispering and pointing at the booth. The glass walls of the ATM were fogged up, and condensation clung to the interior, adding an eerie quality to the scene.

Roshan stepped out of the Jeep, his gaze scanning the area. Patel gestured toward the entrance of the booth, where a forensic team was already at work. Shilpa arrived moments later; her expression grim as she took in the scene.

"Another one," she said softly, falling into step beside Roshan.

"This time it's different," Roshan replied. "An enclosed space as compared to earlier houses. It could explain the use of gas."

They approached the forensic officer, who was dusting the keypad for prints. "What do we know so far?" Roshan asked.

"Ravi Menon entered the booth at around 5:45 AM, according to CCTV footage," the officer said. "He completed a transaction, but something happened inside. The door remained locked, and no one else entered. When the cleaning staff *arrived around 7 AM, they found him collapsed near the machine."*

Roshan glanced at the floor. Ravi Menon's lifeless body had been removed, but the faint outline where he had lain was still visible. He crouched to examine the area, noticing a small, almost imperceptible residue near the fresh air duct.

"The fresh air duct," Roshan said, his voice sharp. "Could gas have been released through there?"

"We're testing for residue," the forensic officer confirmed. "It'll take a few hours, but it's a strong possibility."

Roshan straightened and turned to Patel. "Get a list of everyone who accessed this ATM in the past 48 hours.

And check the surveillance footage again. I want to know if anyone was loitering nearby."

Patel nodded and moved off to coordinate.

Shilpa walked around the booth, her keen eyes scanning the surroundings. She pointed to the crows perched on a nearby lamppost, their black forms stark against the morning light.

"They're here again," she said quietly. "Always watching."

Roshan followed her gaze, his jaw tightening. "It's not a coincidence. They're connected to this. Somehow."

Shilpa turned back to him. "If gas was used, such very small, enclosed space like this would make it lethal in seconds. But how could the killer release it remotely?"

"We're missing something," Roshan admitted. "Let's check the footage."

The police station's surveillance room was dimly lit, the glow of monitors casting harsh shadows on Roshan and Shilpa's faces. The footage from the Street security camera played on a loop. They watched as Ravi Menon entered the booth, inserted his card, and completed a transaction. A few minutes later, he staggered, clutching his throat before collapsing.

"There," Shilpa said, pointing at the screen. "Rewind. Look near the fresh air duct."

Roshan rewound the footage, slowing it down. At the edge of the frame, a crow appeared, landing on the booth's exterior near the fresh air duct. Its head tilted, and it remained there for several seconds before flying off.

Roshan's jaw clenched. "It's the same crow from the Pillai's house footage. Someone's using it. And if it's linked to the gas..." He trailed off, his mind racing.

Later that evening, Roshan decided to confront Martin again. The connection between the murders, the unique moving crow, and the gas residue was too strong to ignore. He arrived at Martin's house as the last light of day faded, casting deep shadows over the neatly trimmed hedges. Martin opened the door with his usual composed smile.

"That crow again," Shilpa murmured. "The same unique movements. It's not natural."

Roshan stepped inside, his gaze scanning the room for anything unusual. "Three people are dead, Martin. And every time, the crows are involved. I can't ignore the connection anymore."

POLICE
ATM
POLICE
POLICE

Martin's smile didn't falter. "Crows are fascinating creatures, aren't they? So intelligent, so adaptable. But you already know that don't you?"

"I know you're hiding something," Roshan said bluntly. "The crows, the timing... it's all too precise. And you seem to have an uncanny interest in these murders."

Martin chuckled softly. "Interest doesn't make me a murderer, Inspector. But tell me... have you ever considered that perhaps the crows aren't the culprits, but the witnesses?"

Roshan stepped closer, his voice low and firm. "What are you trying to say?"

Martin's eyes gleamed in the dim light. "Only that sometimes, the answers are right in front of us, but we're too blind to see them. You're looking at the crows, but perhaps you should be looking at what they're looking at."

Roshan narrowed his eyes. "The crows are always present at the crime scenes, and now you're talking as if you know something more. How do they fit into all of this?"

Martin leaned back slightly, still calm. "Maybe they're just a coincidence. Or maybe they see more than we do. After all, humans are limited by their perception."

Roshan pressed further, pushing the conversation into dangerous territory. "Three murders, Martin. And in all three, the presence of crows coincides with something more sinister. Something invisible."

Martin smirked. "Invisible? Ah, the gas…"

He stopped mid-sentence, but it was too late.

Roshan's expression darkened as he caught the slip. "Gas?" he repeated, his voice sharp.

Martin quickly regained his composure, letting out a soft chuckle. "Inspector, you came here to talk about crows, didn't you? I merely assumed you were considering all possibilities."

*Roshan's voice dropped to a heavy, razor-sharp tone. He didn't blink, his stare locking onto Martin like a predator cornering its prey. **"I NEVER MENTIONED ABOUT THE GAS, MARTIN."***

A moment of silence stretched between them. Martin's smirk faded for a fraction of a second before he leaned forward, regaining control of the conversation. "Come now, Inspector. You're the one who always looks for hidden meanings.

You're investigating something unusual, something unseen—what else could it be? A logical mind considers all angles, does it not?"

Roshan held his ground. "That was more than just a logical guess. You knew, Martin."

Martin exhaled, shaking his head with feigned disappointment. "Roshan, you've always been an interesting man to talk to. But theories aren't proof. And unless you have something concrete, I believe you've overstayed your welcome."

Roshan clenched his jaw. He had rattled Martin, but only briefly. The man was too skilled at deception, too quick at covering his tracks.

Roshan's voice dropped to a low, deliberate tone, laced with quiet menace. He stepped closer, his gaze piercing into Martin's.

"I NEVER MENTIONED THE GAS, MARTIN... YET YOU SPOKE AS IF YOU KNEW THE WHOLE STORY."

His words were heavy, unyielding, hanging in the air like a warning.

"If I find out you're connected to these murders, you'll feel a kind of heat you won't walk away from."

The silence that followed was thick with tension, the weight of his words pressing down like an impending storm.

Martin's smirk returned; his confidence fully restored. "And I'll be watching you, Inspector. Just like the crows."

As Roshan left Martin's house, the weight of his words lingered. The cryptic hints, the unique moving crow, the gas... it all pointed to something larger, something darker. And Roshan knew he was running out of time to uncover the truth.

Chapter 6: The Laboratory in the Forest

Roshan Andreus sat in his office, the glow of the desk lamp illuminating the growing pile of reports and notes that seemed to multiply by the hour. The discovery at the ATM booth had been a breakthrough, but the lack of clear evidence linking the gas and the crow left him restless. He leaned back in his chair, rubbing his temples, when his phone buzzed.

It was Shilpa Narayan. "Roshan, I've been analysing more of the footage from the ATM and the market square," she said. "I found something."

Roshan sat up straight. "Go on."

"There's a pattern to the crow's appearances," Shilpa said. "It's always hovering near structures with ventilation systems or ducts. And I've traced its flight path from the ATM footage. It leads to the edge of the forest."

"The forest?" Roshan repeated, his interest piqued.

"Yes. I did some digging and found out there's an old, abandoned research lab near the area," Shilpa explained. "It's been closed for years, but it might be worth checking out."

Roshan grabbed his notebook. "Send me the coordinates. We'll meet there in an hour."

The forest loomed large and foreboding as Roshan and Patel navigated the winding dirt road leading to the abandoned laboratory. Shilpa arrived shortly after, parking her bike near his Jeep. Together, they made their way through the overgrown path, the silence broken only by the crunch of leaves beneath their feet and the distant cawing of crows.

The laboratory was a dilapidated structure, its once-pristine walls now cracked and covered in moss. Broken windows gaped like empty eye sockets, and the rusted sign at the entrance read, "Dravnika Advanced Research Facility."

"Doesn't look very advanced anymore," Shilpa muttered, adjusting her bag.

Roshan pushed open the creaking metal door, his flashlight cutting through the darkness. Inside, the air was thick with the smell of damp and decay. Papers and equipment lay scattered across the floor, as if whoever had been here last had left in a hurry.

"Look at this," Shilpa said, picking up a faded blueprint from a desk. It showed the layout of a small drone, with annotations detailing its components.

The dim glow of the desk lamp cast eerie shadows across the scattered blueprints and electronic components in the abandoned lab. The air was thick with dust, disturbed only by the occasional flutter of movement from the shattered window, where a lone crow perched, watching.

Roshan stood frozen, his fingers gripping the edges of the brittle blueprint. His pulse pounded in his ears as his eyes scanned the intricate design. The structure was unmistakable wings, a streamlined body, a propulsion system. It wasn't just a drone. It was something far more sinister.

He exhaled sharply; his breath unsteady. "This... this isn't just a surveillance drone," he muttered. "This is a machine designed to blend in."Patel leaned over his shoulder, squinting at the intricate details. "What are you saying, sir?"

Roshan's jaw clenched. He turned the page, revealing another schematic—a detailed rendering of a crow, its skeletal frame eerily mechanical beneath the feathery exterior. His blood ran cold.

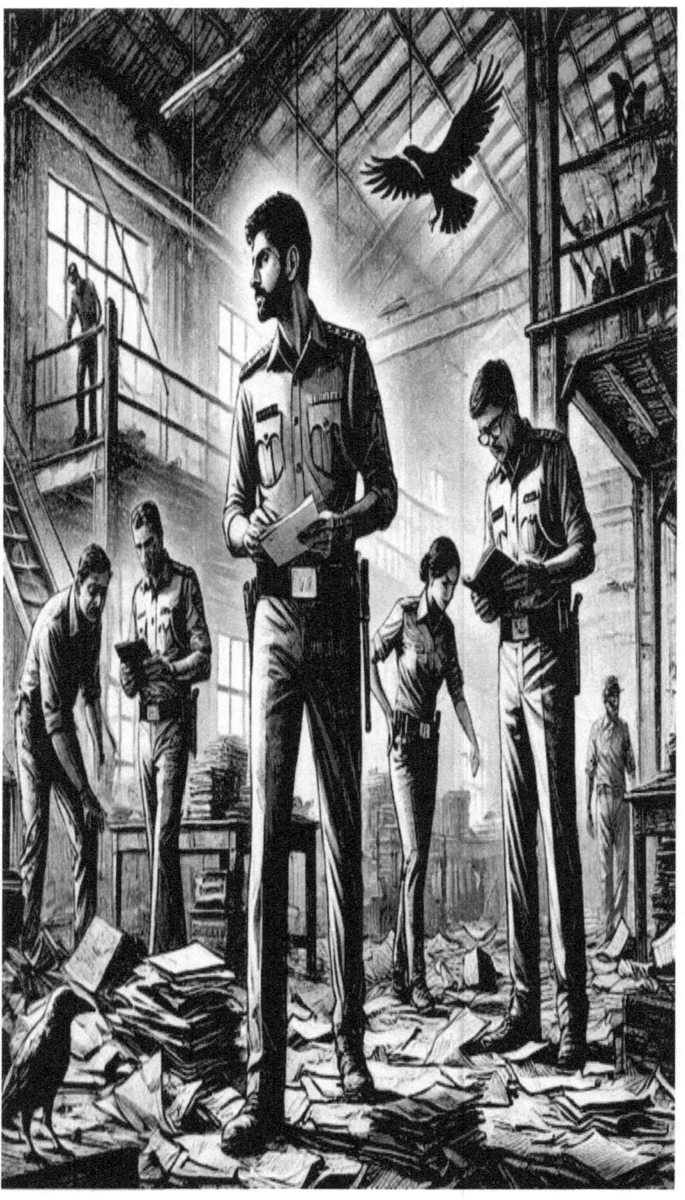

"THIS ISN'T JUST A DRONE,"

Roshan murmured, his grip tightening.

"It's a perfect imitation. A camouflaged machine designed to move, behave, and even perch like a real crow."

Patel's breath hitched. "You mean... all this time, one of those crows wasn't real?"

Roshan's mind raced back to the crime scenes, to the unnatural presence of the crows. The one that moved just a little differently. The one that lingered too long. A horrifying realization sank into his gut like lead.

"They weren't just watching," Roshan said, his voice low and sharp. "They were executing."

The words sent a chill through the room, thick with an unspoken terror. Roshan grabbed the blueprint and held it up to the dim light. The drone's internal structure was mapped with precision—hidden vents, a micro-camera, a controlled dispersal mechanism.

He turned to Patel, his expression dark. "This isn't just about mimicking nature. Someone built these things to kill."

Patel swallowed hard, his throat dry. "Then whoever controls them... they've been at every crime scene."

"But who?" Shilpa asked. "And why?"

Roshan's flashlight landed on a stack of files marked "Project Avian." He opened one, revealing detailed notes on avian behaviour, flight dynamics, and camouflage techniques. "Whoever worked here was studying birds and drones simultaneously," he said. "This wasn't just research. It was development."

"Development for what?" Shilpa asked, her voice uneasy.

Roshan didn't answer. His eyes were fixed on a photo tucked into the file. It showed a group of researchers standing in front of the lab, and among them was a familiar face.

"Martin," Roshan whispered.

Shilpa leaned over to look. "You're sure it's him?"

"I'm certain," Roshan said, his jaw tightening. "He's been lying to us."

The next discovery was even more chilling. In one corner of the lab, they found a locked cabinet. After forcing it open, they uncovered small canisters labelled "Phosgene" and a collection of drone components, including miniature gas dispersal systems.

"This is it," Roshan said, holding up one of the canisters. "This is what's killing them. Phosgene gas, delivered through the "drone" crow."

Shilpa's face paled. "This is military-grade technology. How did Martin get his hands on this?"

As the silence settled, Patel's fingers brushed against another document, partially hidden under a stack of old files. He pulled it free and frowned. "Sir, look at this."

Roshan took the paper and immediately felt a cold prickle down his spine. It was a frequency chart—a log of signals emitted and received by the drone. The pattern was eerily rhythmic, controlled. But what truly unsettled him was the additional data attached.

"These... aren't just signals to control the drone," Roshan muttered. "This is a secondary output. Something is transmitting back."

Patel's eyes widened. "Back to what?"

Roshan's mind worked at lightning speed, piecing together the fragments of the mystery. He flipped through more papers, his breath catching as he saw another diagram—this one of an ultrasonic device embedded within the drone's core structure.

"Sonar manipulation," Roshan whispered. "Low-frequency ultrasonic waves... These drones aren't just blending in with real crows. They're leading them."

Patel's face paled. "You mean the real crows... they're following this thing?"

Roshan nodded grimly. "Whoever designed this knew exactly how crows respond to sound. They're using an ultrasonic frequency—something subtle, just beneath human hearing, but powerful enough to manipulate the flock's behaviour."

*Patel took a step back, his breathing shallow. "That means... wherever the murders happened, the crows didn't just gather by chance. **THEY WERE CALLED THERE.**"*

Roshan slammed the blueprint down. "And whoever's controlling these drones is orchestrating this entire nightmare."

A heavy silence followed, the realization sinking deep. Outside the window, the lone crow flapped its wings once and took off into the night. Roshan's eyes followed its silhouette until it disappeared into the shadows.

He turned back to Patel. "We're not just dealing with a killer. We're dealing with someone who understands the science of control—both human and animal."

His fists clenched. The murders were just the beginning. The real predator was still out there, pulling the strings.

And they had just found their first real lead.

As they left the lab, the cawing of crows grew louder. Dozens of them had gathered in the trees, their black eyes glinting in the fading light. Roshan, Patel and Shilpa quickened their pace, the weight of their discovery pressing down on them.

Back in the Jeep, Roshan told Patel. "Put out an alert for Martin," he said. "We have enough to bring him in for questioning."

"Yes, sir," Patel replied.

Roshan then glanced at Shilpa. "This is bigger than we thought. If Martin's behind this, he's not just a killer. He's a mastermind."

Shilpa nodded, her expression grim. "We need to be careful. If he's gone to these lengths, he won't go down without a fight."

Roshan tightened his grip on the steering wheel. "Then we'll be ready."

Roshan Andreus couldn't shake the image of Martin's face in the old lab photograph. The moment he had seen it, something inside him had clicked—a direct link, undeniable proof that Martin had ties to the abandoned research facility. And if that connection was real, it meant one thing: Martin was more involved in these murders than he was letting on.

Yet, despite this breakthrough, a nagging doubt clawed at the edges of Roshan's mind. Something was missing. A gap in the puzzle, a crucial piece that refused to surface. Why did this all seem too perfect? Why did every step of the investigation feel like it had been laid out in advance, waiting for him to follow?

The drive back to the police station was tense, heavy with unspoken thoughts. The city lights flashed past the windshield in eerie blurs, but

Roshan barely noticed. His mind was a battlefield of logic and suspicion, one moment convinced that he was closing in on the truth, the next fearful that he was being led straight into a trap.

The silence stretched, thick and suffocating, until Shilpa finally spoke.

"We can't arrest him just yet." Her voice was measured, careful. "We need more than circumstantial evidence, Roshan. He's careful... too careful."

Roshan exhaled sharply, gripping the steering wheel tighter. "I know." His jaw clenched, his mind still racing. "But the pieces are starting to fall into place. We just need one break—one solid clue that ties him to the murders."

He stared straight ahead, determination burning behind his eyes. Somewhere in the tangled mess of this case, the answer was waiting. He just had to find it—before it was too late.

Chapter 7: The Fourth Warning

Roshan sat in his dimly lit office, staring at the evidence sprawled across his desk. His mind churned, piecing together fragments of the case—the drone crow, the gas-dispersing mechanism, the ultrasonic generator that manipulated real crows, and the faded group photograph where Martin's face lingered in the background.

Everything was connected, yet something felt... off.

Why did it all come together so easily?

A breakthrough should have felt like victory. Instead, it felt like someone had meticulously written a script, orchestrating every event with chilling precision. Every clue, every turn, every revelation—too seamless, too convenient. It was as if he wasn't uncovering the truth but rather being led down a predetermined path.

A notification flashed on his phone, breaking his thoughts. A text message.

From an unknown number.

"Your time is running out, Inspector. The next victim has already been chosen. You won't be able to save him."

"THE VENUE OF MURDER IS MARKET SQUARE. TOMORROW, 6:00 PM."

"DR. STEPHAN."

Roshan's blood ran cold.

His grip tightened around the phone as his mind raced. This wasn't just another murder waiting to happen. This was a direct challenge. The killer was playing with him, taunting him, daring him to act.

The office door swung open, and Patel rushed in, his face pale.

"Sir," he panted. "We just received an anonymous tip at the station... someone called in—said the next target is Dr. Stephan."

Roshan exhaled sharply. "I already know."

Patel frowned. "How?"

Roshan tossed the phone onto the desk. "Someone is playing with us."

His pulse pounded as he grabbed his coat. This was his chance.

This time, they wouldn't be arriving at a crime scene.

This time, they would prevent one.

As Roshan scrolled through the directory for Dr. Stephan Joseph's contact, his phone rang.

An unknown number flashed on the screen.

He hesitated for a split second before answering.

"Inspector Andreus," a voice on the other end said, low, urgent. "I don't have much time. My name is Dr. Stephan Joseph. I believe I might be Martin's next target."

Roshan's grip on the phone tightened. "Why do you think that? And how is Martin connected?"

Stephan sighed heavily. "It's complicated. But I know Martin. I know what he's capable of. And I know the pattern of the people he's targeting."

Roshan's stomach twisted. "What do you mean, pattern?"

"I can't explain over the phone. Meet me at my clinic. I'll tell you everything. But please... hurry."

Roshan paused, weighing the risk. This could be a trap.

But if he hesitated, Stephan might not live to tell him the truth.

"Fine," Roshan said. "I'll be there in an hour. Don't go anywhere."

Dr. Stephan Joseph's clinic was tucked away on a quiet street, its unassuming exterior hiding the storm brewing inside.

Stephan—a man in his late forties with greying hair and weary eyes—ushered Roshan inside, locking the door behind him.

"Thank you for coming," Stephan said, his voice low. "I don't know where to start, but you need to understand... this isn't random. The people killed...... we're all connected."

Roshan leaned forward, notebook in hand. "Connected how?"

Stephan took a deep breath, his hands trembling slightly. "Years ago, I worked with Martin. Back when he was just a researcher—a brilliant mind obsessed with pushing boundaries. There were five of us in total. Myself, Martin, and three others: Thomas Chacko, Raman Pillai, and Ravi Menon."

Roshan's pulse quickened. "The first three victims."

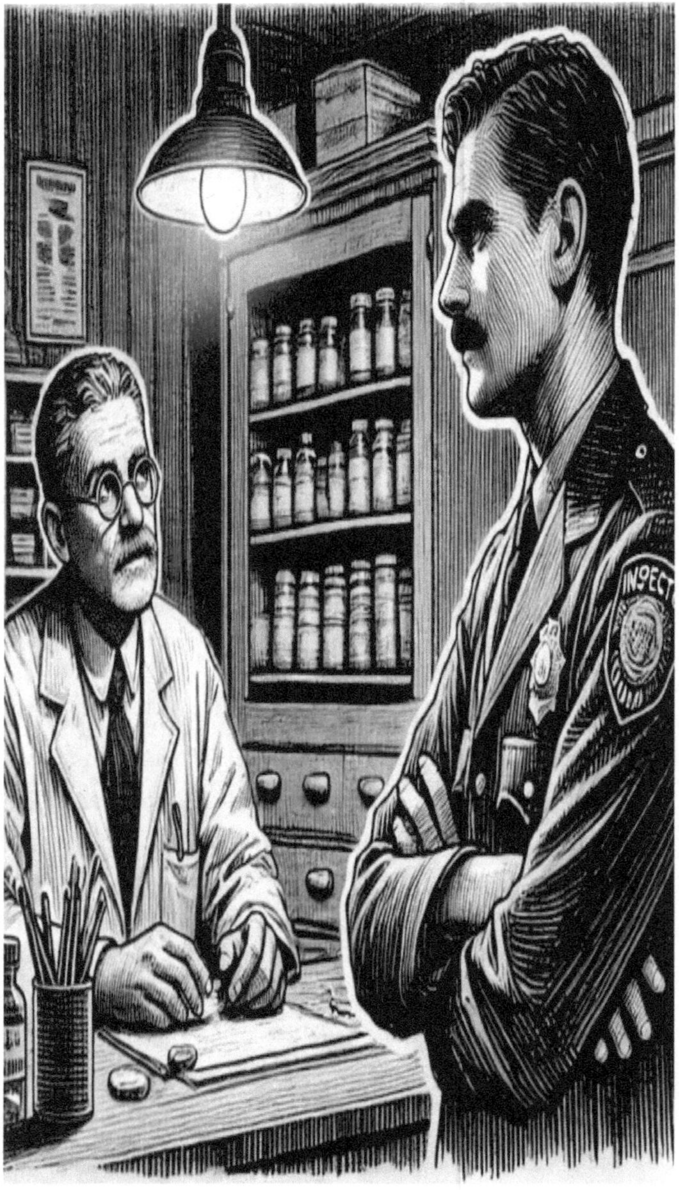

Stephan nodded gravely. "We were part of a project called Avian Dynamics. It was meant to revolutionize surveillance using drones disguised as crows. But Martin... he took it too far. He started experimenting with ways to weaponize them. When we tried to stop him, he vowed revenge. We thought he was just being paranoid... but now?"

Roshan's stomach twisted. "And you are the fifth person?"

Stephan hesitated. "Yes, I think. But I don't think I'm the final target. There's someone else. Someone funded the project. If Martin truly wants to erase the past, he'll go after them too."

"Who?" Roshan pressed.

"I don't know their identity," Stephan admitted. "But I can help you piece it together. I just need your protection."

Roshan exhaled sharply. "Then let's set a trap."

The next day, Market Square buzzed with activity, vendors shouting, people moving in a steady stream.

Dr. Stephan stood in plain sight, appearing vulnerable—but surrounded by plainclothes officers.

Roshan and Patel scanned the sky, waiting for the killer's next move.

Patel gripped the portable signal jammer. "Sir, are you sure this will work?"

"It has to," Roshan muttered. "The drone crow uses electronic signals to control. If we disrupt that... it'll paralyse."

A flock of crows descended, their sharp cries piercing the air.

Roshan narrowed his eyes. Which one was the machine?

The crows moved in harmony, blending seamlessly, making it impossible to tell which was the imposter.

Roshan's frustration boiled over. He glanced at a nearby vendor unloading sacks of rice.

An idea struck him.

He rushed forward, grabbing a handful of rice.

"Spread this on the ground!" he ordered.

The vendor, startled but compliant, did as he was told.

Within seconds, the real crows descended in a frenzy, pecking at the grains.

One crow hovered awkwardly, motionless.

Roshan's eyes locked onto it.

"THAT'S OUR BIRD! ACTIVATE THE JAMMER!"

Patel flipped the switch. A high-frequency pulse rippled through the air.

The robotic crow sputtered, jerking erratically—before crashing onto the pavement.

Officers rushed forward, securing the device. Roshan crouched down, examining it with a mix of triumph and urgency.

He pressed his radio. "I'm sending you the hardware now. Tear it apart—trace its signals. We need to find the source." A voice crackled back. "On it. If this thing is transmitting data, we'll find out were."

As the robotic crow was secured, Roshan felt the first taste of victory.

But deep down, he knew—this was only the beginning.

Somewhere, Martin was watching.

And Roshan knew, with absolute certainty—the mastermind would retaliate.

Chapter 8: The Hunt for the Mastermind

The forensic lab hummed with the low whir of machines, their blinking lights reflecting off metal surfaces.

Roshan stood with his arms crossed, watching as a young man in his late twenties, dressed in a casual hoodie and ripped jeans, hovered over the dismantled robotic crow.

His fingers worked with precision, peeling away layers of synthetic feathers and exposing the intricate circuits beneath.

"Pranav Sharma," Patel muttered, glancing at Roshan. "One of the best in the department when it comes to cybernetics and drone warfare. If anyone can figure this out, it's him."

Pranav didn't look up. "Flattering, but let's stick to business." He tapped a small microchip inside the crow's body, his brow furrowing. "This... this is military-grade tech. Definitely not something a regular tinkerer could whip up in his backyard."

Roshan stepped forward. "Can you trace where it was controlled from?"

Pranav sighed. "That's the problem. The signal was relayed through multiple nodes, bouncing between servers across different locations.

But..." he leaned in, adjusting the magnification on his analysis screen. "There's residual data. Whoever was controlling this, they slipped up. A fragment of a signal is still embedded in the hardware. If I can decrypt it, we might get a location."

Roshan's jaw clenched. "How long?"

Pranav smirked. "Depends on how lucky I get. A few hours. Maybe a day."

Roshan gave a curt nod. "Do it. I need answers."

Roshan had barely stepped out of the lab when his phone buzzed. The screen displayed an unknown number. He answered, his tone sharp. "Who is this?"

A slow chuckle crackled over the line. "Impressive, Inspector. You actually managed to catch my little messenger."

Roshan's grip tightened around the phone. "Hello Martin?"

The voice remained calm, taunting. "You've disrupted my plans, Roshan. That's twice now. But don't feel too proud of yourself... because the game isn't over."

Roshan took a slow breath, forcing his anger to stay in check. "You made a mistake. I have your crow. And soon, I'll have you."

Another laugh, darker this time. "You think so? That's cute. But you're still thinking too small."

Roshan's teeth clenched. "You're running out of time. Surrender now, or—"

"You don't get it, do you?" the voice interrupted, its playful tone vanishing into something colder. "You think you've won? I let you have that crow. It means nothing to me. The fourth act is coming, and this time, you won't stop it."

A chill crept down Roshan's spine. "Fourth act?"

"You should hurry, Inspector. Dr. Stephan might not be so lucky next time."

The line went dead.

Roshan stared at the phone, rage bubbling under his skin. Patel, who had overheard most of the conversation, took a cautious step forward. "Sir... what do we do?"

Roshan's expression hardened. "We don't wait for them to make the next move. We go on the hunt."

Pranav worked tirelessly, his fingers dancing across the keyboard as the decryption program ran lines of code. An hour later, he let out a triumphant grunt. "Got something."

Roshan and Patel rushed over.

Pranav pointed at the screen. "The control signals originated from a relay point inside an abandoned warehouse—just outside the village."

Roshan's eyes darkened. "That's where we go next."

Patel hesitated. "Sir, what if it's a trap?"

Roshan cracked his knuckles. "Then let's make sure we're the ones springing it."

As they gathered their gear, Roshan's mind worked quickly. They needed every possible advantage, and that meant calling in someone who understood the patterns of the crows better than anyone else. He turned to Patel. "Where is Shilpa?"

Patel frowned. "Last I checked, she was at the research centre. Why?"

Roshan didn't answer immediately. Instead, he grabbed his phone and dialled her number. When she picked up, her voice was neutral. "Roshan?"

"I need you on this one, Shilpa." There was a pause. "Why?"

"Because we're going in blind," Roshan admitted. "The crows weren't just a coincidence at the crime scenes. They were manipulated, controlled. If there's any defensive mechanism or pattern in how they behave, I need you to recognize it before we walk into another trap."

Shilpa exhaled softly. "You're finally trusting me on this?"

Roshan's grip tightened around the phone. "I need you to see things I can't."

Another pause. Then, "Fine. I'll meet you at the rendezvous point."

As they gathered their team and prepped for the mission, the weight of the final confrontation settled over them. The mastermind was still out there, taunting them, daring them to stop the inevitable. But Roshan had had enough of playing defence.

It was time to end this.

Chapter 9: The Mask Falls

The abandoned warehouse loomed ahead, its rusted steel beams jutting out like skeletal remains against the night sky. The dim glow of the moon barely illuminated the cracked concrete ground, and the thick silence was occasionally broken by the distant cawing of crows. A chilling reminder of what lay ahead.

Roshan crouched near the entrance, his sharp eyes scanning the building's perimeter. Patel knelt beside him, checking his weapon, while Pranav adjusted his handheld scanner. Shilpa stood slightly apart; her gaze locked on the warehouse's looming darkness. The weight of her presence was unsettling, but Roshan pushed that thought aside.

"This is it," Roshan murmured, gripping his pistol tighter. "We move in, sweep the area, and find the control centre. No mistakes."

Patel gave a nod, his jaw tight. "And if Martin's inside?"

Roshan's expression hardened. "Then we end this tonight."

With precision, the team moved. The door creaked as Roshan pushed it open, the sound echoing through the vast emptiness inside. Shafts of moonlight filtered through the broken ceiling, casting eerie patterns across rusted machinery and stacks of wooden crates.

Pranav's scanner beeped faintly, displaying flickering signals. "There's definitely a control system somewhere inside," he whispered. "Strong signal ahead."

Roshan gestured for the team to split—Patel and two officers sweeping the left flank, Pranav and another officer covering the right. He moved ahead with Shilpa, his instincts prickling at the silence.

Something wasn't right.

They navigated through the maze of debris, their footsteps carefully measured. A faint hum vibrated through the air—subtle, but unmistakable.

"There," Shilpa whispered, pointing to a makeshift console set against the far wall. The monitors flickered with encrypted data, a network of surveillance feeds, and—more chillingly—a real-time control interface for the drone crows.

Roshan's grip tightened on his pistol as he scanned the darkness. Where was Martin?

A slow clap echoed through the cavernous space.

"Inspector Andreus," Martin's voice rang out, smooth as silk. "How predictable."

Martin emerged from the shadows, his figure illuminated by a faint overhead light, moving with effortless confidence with a pistol in hand. Dressed in his signature white attire, his expression carried an air of amused indifference.

*The warehouse was eerily silent, the dim overhead lights flickering as Roshan and Shilpa stepped forward, their eyes locked onto **Martin**, who stood calmly in the centre of the vast open space.*

*A faint smirk played on Martin's lips as he **spread his arms in a mock gesture of welcome**. "Inspector Andreus. And Shilpa. What a pleasure."*

*Roshan's eyes burned with unrelenting focus. "**It ends tonight, Martin.**"*

*Martin chuckled, his expression amused. "**Oh, Roshan, you always say that. Yet, here we are. Again.**"*

*Shilpa's fists clenched at her sides, but before she could speak, **a distant burst of gunfire*** *echoed through the warehouse,* followed by the explosion.

Roshan's jaw tightened. **Patel's team. They were engaging Martin's men elsewhere.**

Martin's eyes glinted as he **tilted his head toward the commotion.** *"Ah, sounds like my boys are keeping your friends busy."*

Roshan didn't take the bait.

Martin sighed, looking between them. **"So, tell me. What's the plan, Roshan? You shoot me? Arrest me? Hope I beg for mercy?"**

Roshan's grip on his gun **tightened. "The only thing I hope for, Martin, is that you don't walk out of here."**

Martin let out a **low, appreciative whistle. "Now that's the spirit."** *Then,* **he moved—fast.**

With blinding speed, **Martin lunged forward,** *his fist swinging toward Roshan's ribs* **with brutal force.**

Roshan barely managed to **twist his body,** *dodging at the last second, but* **Martin's knee drove into his stomach,** *knocking the breath from his lungs.*

Roshan recovered just in time to see **Martin step between Roshan and Shilpa, separating them like a predator dividing its prey.**

Martin turned to Roshan, **smirking. "You should have brought backup."**

Roshan wiped the blood from the corner of his mouth and **spat onto the ground. "I didn't need any."**

Martin chuckled, rolling his shoulders. **"Well, that was a mistake."**

Then, he attacked again.

Roshan gritted his teeth, pain rippling through his torso as he staggered back, trying to regain control. But Martin wasn't done. With predatory instincts, he pivoted, his body coiling like a spring before he lashed out again—this time, his elbow driving directly into Roshan's left arm with bone-crushing force.

A sickening crack echoed through the dimly lit room.

Roshan barely had time to register the sharp, unbearable agony shooting through his arm before he realized—his left hand was no longer responding.

His fingers trembled, his forearm limp, useless. A wave of blinding pain surged through his nerves, momentarily stunning him.

Martin's lips curled into a wicked smirk. "You're slowing down, Inspector," he taunted, circling him like a vulture sensing weakness.

Roshan forced himself to focus, his vision blurring slightly from the pain. He attempted to raise his gun with his right hand, but before he could steady it, Martin struck again—this time a sharp kick to Roshan's wrist.

The gun wrenched free from his grip, spinning through the air before clattering against the cold, dusty floor, Stopping just inches away from Shilpa.

Roshan's pulse pounded in his ears as he looked up, his gaze locking onto hers. His mind raced, the pain throbbing through his arm, but a deeper, more paralyzing fear settled in.

Martin straightened, dusting off his sleeve. "See? That's the problem with you, Roshan. You always think you're in control."

Roshan's gaze snapped toward Shilpa. "Shilpa... the gun."

She stood still; her expression unreadable as she stared at the firearm near her feet.

"Pick it up," Roshan said, his voice urgent.

For a moment, time seemed to freeze.

*Then, Shilpa slowly bent down, her fingers wrapping around the handle of the gun. She straightened, holding it firmly. Her steps were slow, deliberate, as she moved towards not to rishan but towards **MARTIN**.....*

Roshan's chest tightened. "Shilpa... what are you doing?"

Martin's smirk widened as Shilpa came to a halt beside him. Then, with a practiced ease, she raised the gun.

And pointed it at Roshan.

A cold shiver ran down Roshan's spine. "No," he breathed, his eyes locking onto hers. "Shilpa... don't."

Her grip on the gun tightened. Her voice was barely above a whisper. "I have to."

Martin placed a hand on Shilpa's shoulder, his expression triumphant. "She was never truly with you Roshan"

Roshan's fists clenched. "Shilpa, you don't have to do this."

Shilpa's **eyes wavered for just a second**. Then— **she stepped back toward Martin.**

Martin's smirk widened. **Slowly, deliberately, he turned to face Roshan, savoring the moment.**

He let out a low chuckle, shaking his head in **mock sympathy. "Oh, Roshan... that look on your face. The realization. The pain. The betrayal. Beautiful."**

He clapped his hands together—**a slow, theatrical applause.**

"What a performance, Shilpa. What a masterpiece." He turned slightly, eyeing her with approval. **"I always knew you had it in you. But this? This is legendary."**

Roshan's **fists clenched, his knuckles white**. His breath was **ragged with fury,** but his body remained stone still, processing what just happened.

Martin's gaze **flicked back to Roshan**, his voice laced with triumph.

"You fought so hard for her. You trusted her. And now? She belongs to me."

He took a slow step forward. **"Tell me, Inspector, how does it feel? Knowing that everything you stood for, everything you believed in—was nothing but an illusion?"**

Roshan's **jaw tightened**, his entire body burning with restrained rage. **"Shilpa, don't do this."**

But Shilpa didn't respond. She only **lowered her gaze**.

Martin let out a small **mocking sigh**, shaking his head. **"Oh, come now, Roshan. Don't take it personally. Some people are just... destined to stand on the winning side."**

He turned toward Shilpa, **his voice turning softer, yet commanding. "And you, my dear, have just secured your place."**

Shilpa remained still, **her expression unreadable.**

Martin grinned, looking back at Roshan. **"Take a good look, Inspector. This is what true victory looks like."**

Roshan wiped the blood from his lip, his gaze sharp despite the pain.

Martin chuckled, stepping forward, his voice dripping with amusement.

But let's be honest, Roshan... you're always one step too late. Always reacting. Always chasing. Tell me—when was the last time you were actually in control?"

Roshan exhaled, shaking his head. **"You talk too much, Martin."**

Martin grinned, his eyes gleaming with amusement. **"And you fight too hard for a game you've already lost."**

Roshan took a **slow, deliberate step forward,** ignoring the searing pain in his body. **"Then finish it."**

Martin raised a brow. **"What?"**

Roshan **locked eyes with him,** his voice low and menacing. **"If you don't want to get killed, do it now. Put a bullet in me and walk away. Because if you don't—if you let me live—I swear on** *everything you hold dear... you will not walk this earth much longer."*

*Martin's smirk faltered **just for a second** before it returned, wider than before. **"Now that's the fire I wanted to see."***

*He leaned in slightly, lowering his voice. **"You think you can stop me, Roshan? You? A man barely breathing, barely standing?"***

*Roshan **didn't blink. "Try me."***

*Martin studied him for a moment, then let out a soft laugh. **"Not yet. You see, killing you now? That would be mercy. But watching you break? Watching you crawl, knowing that no matter what you do, you'll never be fast enough, never be smart enough to stop me? That's the real game."***

*Roshan **clenched his jaw, fury burning in his veins.***

*Martin took a step back, still smiling. **"I'll see you soon, Inspector. If you're still alive by then."***

"Time to go."

A signal. A trigger.

*Within seconds, smoke erupted into the room, gunfire crackling in the distance. Martin **turned*** *sharply, gripping Shilpa's arm as they disappeared into the chaos—leaving Roshan standing there, helpless, defeated... but burning with a vengeance that would not die.*

*As the **smoke curled through the warehouse**, Roshan **steadied himself**, his body aching, his gun trembling in his grip.*

When the light faded, they were gone.

Patel rushed to the room and help Roshan, gripping his uninjured arm. "Sir, we need to get you out of here."

Roshan forced himself to his feet, breathing heavily. His mind raced, replaying every interaction with Shilpa, every moment he had trusted her. It had all been a lie.

Pranav entered into the room and said "The system's data been wiped. We lost our best lead."

Roshan's hands curled into fists. His blood pounded in his ears, drowning out everything but one thought:

This wasn't over. He staggered toward the exit, every step fuelled by sheer will. "No more playing their game," he growled. "We take the fight to them."

As the remaining officers secured the warehouse, the night air buzzed with an unshakable tension.

Martin and Shilpa had won this round.

But Roshan wasn't finished yet.

Chapter 10: Shadows of the Past

The cold silence of the hideout was only broken by the rhythmic tapping of Martin's fingers against the armrest of his chair. A bottle of whiskey sat untouched on the wooden table, next to a small stack of cash. Across from him, Shilpa sat with her hands clasped, staring at the floor, lost in thought.

"You look troubled," Martin mused, his voice smooth as ever. "Regretting your choices?"

Shilpa's jaw tightened. "I didn't have a choice."

Martin chuckled. "Oh, but you did. You could've walked away. But instead, here you are." He leaned forward. "You were always smart, Shilpa. You knew how to play the game. So why do you look like you've lost?"

Shilpa's gaze flickered up to meet his. "Because I didn't expect it to go this far."

Flashback: How It All Began

An **year ago**, Shilpa had been drowning in **debt**, struggling to keep herself afloat as the weight of her father's medical bills **crushed her spirit**. The once-lively house she had grown up in had *become **a battlefield of survival**, where every conversation with her father revolved around **medications, hospital visits, and their dwindling finances.***

*She had tried **everything**—working **overtime**, selling **whatever she could**, even skipping meals to ensure her father **had his treatment**. But it was never enough.*

*"**Don't worry about me, mol,**" her father had said, his frail hand clasping hers. "**I'll be fine. You've done enough.**"*

*But Shilpa **knew it was a lie**. His breathing had grown **shallower**, his once-commanding voice now a mere whisper. The doctors had been clear—**without proper treatment, his time was limited.***

*The **banks had refused her requests** for an extension, the creditors had **stopped being patient**, and the **landlord had hinted at eviction**. Every door she knocked on had closed in her face.*

*She had spent **nights awake**, staring at the ceiling, wondering how much longer she could **keep fighting** before she lost everything.*

*And then—**Martin entered her life.***

It had been an expensive café—**the kind she would never have stepped into willingly**, but that day, she had been desperate. A friend had suggested a potential investor willing to help.

She had been expecting a **businessman, a loan officer, anyone—but not Martin.**

The **moment he walked in**, his presence had been **imposing yet effortless**. A crisp white shirt, an air of quiet confidence, a **predatory grace hidden behind a charming smile**. He had moved with **purpose**, and before she could even process it, he had slid into the seat across from her.

"I hear you need help," he had said smoothly, setting his coffee cup down with an air of complete control.

Shilpa had **stiffened**, her instincts screaming that this was **a man who didn't just offer help—he demanded something in return.**

"Who are you?" she had asked, her voice guarded.

Martin had simply **tilted his head, studying her** like she was a puzzle he already knew how to solve.

"Let's just say... I know a thing or two about difficult choices."

And that was how it had begun.

*A **conversation** that had felt like a negotiation, a chess game where **she was already losing before she had even moved a piece.***

*And by the time the coffee had gone cold—**she had already signed an invisible deal with the devil.***

At first, it was small things—monitoring certain people, feeding Martin information. It seemed harmless. Until it wasn't.

When she had realized who he truly was, it was too late.

She had tried to leave. Tried to fight back.

But Martin had been one step ahead. "You owe me, Shilpa," he had reminded her. "And in my world, debts don't just disappear."

*So, she had **been forced to stay** against her will*

Back to the Present

Shilpa exhaled, rubbing her temples. "You forced me into this."

Martin smirked. "Did I? Or did I simply open a door you were too afraid to walk through?"

She didn't answer. Because the truth was, a part of her had wanted the security Martin had offered. Even now, despite everything, she wasn't sure if she had any way out.

Martin leaned back. "Enough reminiscing. We need to focus on what comes next."

Shilpa looked at him warily. "Stephan."

Martin nodded. "Roshan was supposed to be blindsided by your betrayal. But he's smarter than I gave him credit for. That means we can't afford mistakes."

Shilpa swallowed. "You want me to do it, don't you?"

Martin raised an eyebrow. "Would that be a problem?"

She hesitated. "I... I didn't sign up for this."

Martin's eyes darkened. "You signed up for whatever I tell you to do."

Shilpa's stomach churned, but she knew there was no arguing. Not with him.

Meanwhile, back at the police station, Roshan sat in his office, his fingers drumming against the desk. A thick plaster was wrapped tightly around his upper arm, supporting his wounded shoulder, but the dull ache persisted with every small movement. He ignored the pain, his mind elsewhere—on Shilpa, on Martin, on what came next.

Patel stood by the door. "Sir, we've been searching every known safe house Martin's used before, but he's gone completely off-grid."

Roshan clenched his jaw. "Then we stop looking in obvious places."

Pranav, sitting in front of his laptop, glanced up. "What do you mean?"

Roshan stood, grabbing a marker and moving to the whiteboard. He circled several locations on the map. "Martin's smart. He knows we're looking at his old patterns. So, he's doing something different."

Pranav frowned. "But where would he go?"

Roshan tapped a spot on the board. "Somewhere that doesn't tie back to him.

Somewhere only his newest recruit would know."

Patel's eyes widened. "Shilpa."

Roshan nodded. "She's been with him for months. She knows his recent movements, his recent contacts. If she wanted to disappear with him, she'd choose somewhere new."

Pranav smirked. "And you have a plan, don't you?"

Roshan's lips curled into a dangerous smile. "Of course. We're going to use her own past against her."

Roshan's team moved swiftly. Through bank records, call logs, and hidden surveillance, they retraced Shilpa's steps over the last few months. Pranav hacked into her encrypted files, uncovering emails and transactions that pointed to a remote villa outside the city.

Patel checked his gun. "If they're there, what's the plan?"

Roshan's expression was steel. "We don't storm in. We wait. We make them think they're safe.

And when they least expect it..." he smirked, "we take them down."

Pranav nodded. "And what about Shilpa?"

Roshan exhaled. "She made her choice."

Patel hesitated. "You don't believe that."

His mind was a battlefield—**Shilpa's betrayal replaying like a relentless echo**. Every moment, every conversation he had shared with her now felt like a lie, a script written long before he ever stepped into this deadly game.

His fingers **tightened into fists**, his nails digging into his palms as he exhaled sharply.

Why, Shilpa? Why?

As if the universe had heard his thoughts, **his phone vibrated in his pocket.**

A **single notification**.

His **blood turned cold** when he saw the sender's name.

Shilpa.

His heart pounded. **She had messaged him.**

Roshan grabbed his phone, his fingers trembling slightly as he swiped it open.

One unread WhatsApp message.

*The moment he clicked it, the message **vanished** before his eyes.*

An auto-delete message.

*Roshan's breath hitched. **What the hell—?***

But his phone had caught a preview before it disappeared. He blinked at the fragment still lingering on the notification bar.

"Sorry... I never wanted this to happen. But it just... happened."

*His pulse **roared in his ears**. His chest felt tight, the world around him shrinking to just that one sentence.*

Then another preview flashed.

***"Be careful, Martin is dangerous..."** then the message got deleted immediately.*

*Roshan **froze**. His mind refused to process it.*

*His hands clenched the phone so hard **his knuckles turned white**.*

Shilpa. This wasn't a betrayal.

This was a warning. For the first time since she had pointed that gun at him, **Roshan felt the truth clawing its way into his gut.**

She hadn't chosen Martin. She had been forced into his web.

Roshan exhaled, his jaw tightening.

This wasn't just about **justice anymore.**

This was **personal.** Martin had played him—**but Shilpa?**

She was **still in the game.** And **if she was warning him, then she wasn't truly lost yet.**

His grip loosened slightly, his breath steadying. His mind was already **moving, planning, calculating.**

Now, it was Roshan's turn to strike.

Chapter 11: The Final Confrontation

The night was thick with tension. The air inside the SUV felt electric as Roshan, Patel, and Pranav sat in silence, the weight of what was about to unfold pressing against them. Pranav's fingers danced over the keyboard, decrypting the last known locations tied to Shilpa's movements over the past few months.

"There," Pranav finally said, his voice firm, pointing at a blinking dot on the satellite map. "A private estate, deep in the hills, completely isolated."

Roshan's eyes narrowed as he studied the screen. "That's where they are."

Patel nodded. "And we're going in."

Roshan took a deep breath, his mind racing. They weren't walking into this blindly. They had learned from past mistakes. This time, they would strike first.

"Listen up," Roshan said, his voice sharp, commanding. "We hit them hard, no warning, no hesitation. Martin is dangerous, and Shilpa... we don't know where she stands anymore."

Pranav looked up. "Do we try to bring her back?"

Roshan hesitated. "If she gives us a reason, yes. But we don't risk the mission for her."

Patel exhaled. "Then let's end this."

The convoy of police vehicles moved under the cover of darkness, their lights off, engines low. The estate loomed ahead; an imposing structure surrounded by dense forest.

Roshan signalled the team. "Positions."

Patel and the assault unit spread out, taking vantage points around the perimeter. Pranav stayed back in the tech van, monitoring security feeds, whispering updates through the earpiece.

Roshan's heart pounded as he reached the main entrance, his gun steady. He motioned to Patel. "On my mark."

A deep breath.

"Go!"

The door burst open, and the team flooded in. Gunfire erupted as Martin's men retaliated, bullets tearing through furniture and glass. Smoke filled the air.

The battlefield of shattered glass and echoes of gunfire had stilled, but the tension in the air was suffocating. The sound of heavy breathing and distant footsteps faded as Roshan scanned the dimly lit corridor, his senses sharp, his heartbeat thundering in his ears.

Then, amidst the chaos—

"Roshan."

That voice.

Roshan's blood turned to ice.

He turned slowly, his grip tightening around his gun as his gaze lifted towards the grand staircase.

There, bathed in the eerie glow of flickering light, stood Martin—calm, composed, and in complete control. His lips curled into that signature smirk, the devil's grin that had haunted Roshan for too long.

And in front of him, trembling, barely able to breathe, was Shilpa.

A sharp blade pressed against her throat, the silver glinting menacingly under the dim light.

Her wide eyes locked onto Roshan's, filled with a desperate plea.

A silent scream.

Martin's voice was almost a purr. "Drop your weapons, Inspector. Or she dies."

The words slithered through the air, sinking their venom into Roshan's spine. His hands trembled ever so slightly, but his gun remained raised, locked onto Martin's smug face.

"Let her go," Roshan growled, his voice thick with restrained rage. "This is over."

Martin's chuckle was soft, almost amused. "Over? Oh, Roshan... we haven't even reached the climax yet."

Shilpa drew in a shaky breath, her body tensing under Martin's unyielding grasp. "Roshan..." her voice trembled, barely audible. "This was never my choice.

"Quiet," Martin hissed, his fingers pressing deeper against her skin.

Roshan's mind raced. One wrong move and Martin would slit her throat in an instant. Every scenario ran through his mind, every possible opening—but the margin of error was too thin.

Shilpa suddenly took a slow, shuddering breath. Her lips quivered, and then—

"I'm sorry," she whispered, her voice cracking.

Martin rolled his eyes. "Oh, how touching. Regrets, confessions—go on, make it dramatic."

But Roshan wasn't looking at Martin anymore. His focus was entirely on Shilpa, his pulse hammering. "Shilpa, don't—"

She slowly shook her head, her eyes glistening with unshed tears. "I... I was blind. I let him manipulate me. But not anymore."

Martin's smirk faltered. "What the hell are you doing?"

Roshan took a slow step forward. "Shilpa, don't do anything stupid."

She exhaled shakily. "I already did."

She closed her eyes for a fraction of a second, then met Roshan's gaze again. "I'm the reason you hesitated," she said, her voice breaking. "I'm the reason you can't act now. If I remain here... you'll never be able to stop him."

Roshan's breath caught. "Don't say that."

She offered him a fragile, bittersweet smile, her eyes glistening with regret. "Then I'll say this—I **WON'T BE THE REASON HE WINS.**" She swallowed hard, her voice cracking.

"AND I'M SORRY, ROSHAN... FOR EVERYTHING. FOR BETRAYING YOU....

Martin's grip tightened. "Shilpa, what the hell are you—"

And before anyone could react, Shilpa made her choice.

With a sudden, deliberate motion, she surged forward driving herself straight into the waiting blade.

A horrifying, wet slick echoed through the room as the steel tore through her flesh. Her body convulsed violently in Martin's grip, a sharp, ragged gasp escaping her lips as searing pain consumed her. Warm, thick blood gushed from the wound, spreading in dark, crimson streaks across Martin's pristine white shirt, staining it like a mark of his sins.

Time slowed.

"No!" Roshan roared, his world tilting into a blur.

Martin's eyes widened in sheer disbelief, his grip loosening as Shilpa crumbled in his arms. Her hands clutched at the wound, her breaths coming in ragged gasps, but her eyes—her eyes remained locked on Roshan.

She tried to smile. "Finish this," she whispered, her body giving way, slipping from Martin's grip.

Roshan's fury ignited. A fire unlike anything he had ever felt before.

Martin staggered back; his hands drenched in Shilpa's blood. For the first time, his unshakable confidence faltered. His fingers trembled as he looked down at the crimson staining his white shirt, his breath ragged. Panic flickered in his dark eyes—a stark contrast to the smug arrogance he had worn moments ago.

"Damn it... DAMN IT!" he bellowed, his voice laced with desperation, the realization of his own mortality gripping him like a vice.

Roshan didn't hesitate.

Time seemed to slow. Every heartbeat thundered in his ears; every fibre of his being focused on a single action.

With blinding speed, he pulled the trigger.

The gunshot tore through the suffocating silence, the muzzle flash illuminating the darkened room like a burst of fire. The bullet slammed into Martin's chest, the impact forcing him backward. His body jerked violently, his mouth parting in a strangled gasp. His fingers *clawed at the gaping wound, as if he could grasp onto life itself, refusing to let go.*

He stumbled, his knees giving way, his once-arrogant smirk now twisted into an agonized grimace. Blood trickled from the corner of his lips, staining his teeth as he coughed. He let out a weak, bitter chuckle, a final, hollow remnant of the man who thought himself untouchable.

"So... you finally did it." His voice was hoarse, barely above a whisper.

Roshan's boots echoed against the cold concrete floor as he stepped forward, his gun still raised, his gaze unflinching. The fire in his eyes was no longer fuelled by rage—it was something darker, something final.

"She gave you everything," Roshan said, his voice sharp as a blade, slicing through the heavy air. "And you used her."

Martin let out another ragged breath, his body swaying. His smirk, though fading, never fully disappeared. His gaze flickered up to Roshan, his lips curling into something that resembled amusement, even in the face of death.

"And you... let her die."

Roshan's hands curled into fists, his knuckles whitening under the pressure. His grip on the gun remained firm, but his entire body tensed at those words. His chest heaved, his mind screaming at him that this wasn't his fault—that Shilpa had made her choice. And yet...

"No." Roshan's voice was steady, unwavering. "You killed her the moment you made her choose."

Martin exhaled one last chuckle, but before it could fully leave his lips—

Roshan pulled the trigger again.

The final shot echoed like thunder.

Martin's body jerked once before he crumpled lifelessly to the ground, collapsing beside Shilpa. His open eyes stared into nothingness; his reign of control shattered in a single moment.

For a long moment, there was only silence. The battle was over. But Roshan felt no victory.

Chapter:12 The Aftermath

The silence that followed was deafening.

The team stormed in, but Roshan barely registered them. His steps were heavy, numb, as he dropped to his knees beside Shilpa's still body.

Patel approached cautiously; his voice hesitant. "Sir... it's over."

Roshan exhaled shakily. "No. It will never be over."

He knelt closer, brushing a strand of hair from Shilpa's blood-streaked face. "I should have saved you," he whispered, guilt crushing him.

Pranav stood at the doorway; his face solemn. "She saved you."

Roshan didn't reply.

Instead, he closed his eyes, letting the weight of everything sink in.

The Whispering Crows had finally gone silent.

But at what cost?

The cold grey walls of the Commissioner's office loomed around Roshan as he stood at attention, his uniform crisp but weighed down by the exhaustion of the past few days. The air inside was heavy with silence, broken only by the faint hum of the ceiling fan. Commissioner Menon sat behind his large wooden desk, fingers steepled, his piercing eyes fixed on Roshan.

"Sit," Menon ordered, his voice devoid of emotion.

Roshan lowered himself into the chair, the weight of the case pressing against his chest. Across the table, Deputy Commissioner Rana flipped through the case files, his brows furrowed in concentration.

"Start from the beginning," Menon said, leaning forward slightly. "I want everything."

Roshan exhaled; his voice steady but drained. "Thomas Chacko, Raman Pillai, and Ravi Menon were all part of an advanced research initiative alongside Stephan and Martin. The project initially had noble intentions—developing drone technology integrated with avian behaviour for environmental monitoring and surveillance. However, as the research progressed, Martin had other plans. He saw the potential of weaponizing their findings for far more sinister purposes."

Roshan paused, his fists clenching slightly before he continued. "The turning point came when Martin initiated cross-country negotiations, attempting to sell their breakthrough technology to underground networks. He was in talks with foreign defence contractors, espionage agencies, and even criminal syndicates who saw the potential of a virtually undetectable assassination tool. When the others—Chacko, Pillai, and Ravi Menon—realized the direction Martin was taking, they resisted. They refused to turn their life's work into a tool for mass murder."

Roshan's voice grew sharper. "But Martin wasn't someone who accepted defiance. He saw them as liabilities, men who could expose his dealings, ruin his ambitions. And so, he orchestrated their deaths, eliminating them one by one. He weaponized their own creation—deploying a drone-operated system that mimicked the natural movement of crows, using the birds to release a lethal gas in precise, controlled attacks. His method was flawless, undetectable. He believed he was above the law, beyond our reach."

Menon nodded slowly, his fingers tapping against the desk. "And Shilpa Narayan?"

Roshan's jaw tightened. "She was manipulated. A pawn in his game. She betrayed us, but in the end... she tried to make things right."

Deputy Commissioner Rana, who had been silently flipping through the case files, looked up. "And how do you justify her actions? She actively aided a criminal."

Roshan met his gaze firmly. "She did. But she also sacrificed herself to stop him. She realized too late what she had become, and she paid the ultimate price."

The room fell into silence. The weight of those words hung heavy in the air.

Menon leaned back, exhaling deeply. "And Martin?"

Roshan's eyes darkened. "Dead."

Rana closed the file with a soft thud. "So, it's over."

Roshan shook his head. "The case is closed, but it's never really over, sir. The people Martin hurt, the lives he destroyed... that damage doesn't just disappear." He let out a slow breath. "But justice has been served."

Menon studied Roshan for a long moment before nodding. "You did well, Inspector. Your methods were unconventional, but you got the job done."

Roshan didn't respond. The victory felt hollow.

Menon stood, extending his hand. "Take a few days off, Roshan. Get some rest."

Roshan hesitated before shaking his superior's hand. "Thank you, sir."

As he left the office, stepping into the cool evening air, Roshan looked up at the sky. The crows that had once loomed over Dravnika's darkness were gone, the night strangely quiet.

The whispering crows had finally fallen silent.

And so had the storm.

Roshan sat in his dimly lit apartment; his body weary but his mind restless. He poured himself a glass of whiskey, staring at the golden liquid swirling inside, but never drinking. The weight of everything pressed down on him—Martin's twisted vision, Shilpa's sacrifice, the countless lives lost.

The city outside was quiet, unnaturally so.

Then, a sound.

A soft flutter.

Roshan turned his head sharply towards the window.

A crow sat perched on the ledge.

But something was off.

Its movements were too precise. Too mechanical. Its head tilted at an unnatural angle, its cold, unblinking eyes locked onto Roshan.

Roshan's fingers instinctively reached for his gun, his pulse spiking. The dim glow of the streetlight caught a glint of metal beneath the bird's feathers.

A ROBOTIC CROW...........

His breath hitched as realization settled in. Martin was gone, but his technology—his legacy—was not.

*As Roshan stared at the silent machine watching him, a single thought ran through his mind, sending a chill down his spine.The crows were still **WHISPERING....***

And the storm was far from over

---

www.ingramcontent.com/pod-product-compliance
Lightning Source LLC
Chambersburg PA
CBHW031259130726
47988CB00007B/2648